To Penelope and Felicity, who taught us that you are ABLE to do
anything if you are kind, brave, and true to yourself
Love, Mommy & Daddy

Text copyright © 2022 by Korey Watari
Illustrations copyright © 2022 by Mike Wu
All rights reserved.

No part of this book may be reproduced, or stored in a retrieval system, or transmitted in any form or by any means,
electronic, mechanical, photocopying, recording, or otherwise, without express written permission of the publisher.

Published by Two Lions, New York
www.apub.com
Amazon, the Amazon logo, and Two Lions are trademarks of Amazon.com, Inc., or its affiliates.

Author's note photograph by Henry Watari.

ISBN-13: 9781542031530 • ISBN-10: 1542031532

The illustrations were rendered in watercolors, sumi brush, pencil, and digital media.
Book design by Abby Dening

Printed in China
First Edition
1 3 5 7 9 10 8 6 4 2

I Am Able to
SHINE

BY **Korey Watari**   ILLUSTRATED BY **Mike Wu**

two lions

Eiko has a spirited soul and a head full of ideas.
Each night she whispers to her crane,

"I wish . . .

Her generous heart fills her with strength and purpose.
She sprinkles friendship all around.

She is KIND.

Keiko sometimes feels invisible.

"Chin up, Keiko! One step is all it takes,"

she reminds herself.

She PERSEVERES.

Kalamazoo

At times Keiko wants to be
someone else.

She often wonders,

"Why can't others see me
the way I do?
I am a good person."

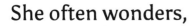

She is DETERMINED.

As the sun rises and falls,
Keiko's family surrounds her with love.

"Keiko-chan, remember that you are always able to SHINE, no matter what anyone else thinks,"

they tell her.

She is LOVED.

People may misjudge her. They may even be unkind.
Keiko remains steady like a tree.

She is able to stand STRONG.

As Keiko blossoms, her confidence ignites.

She believes in herself and opens her heart.

She is able to INSPIRE.

Keiko celebrates her differences and discovers
a beautiful spirit can shine on the outside too.

She is able to give HOPE.

Keiko is proud that her eyes are shaped like
crescent moons and her hair is dark as night.
Her soul is the richest color of all.

She is able to
OVERCOME.

She is no longer afraid to raise her voice, share her doubts, or express her frustration.

She is COURAGEOUS.

Keiko learns to love herself and declares,

"I am beautiful.

In time she will share herself with the world
and be inspired by what she finds.

She will LEAD.

One day she will receive one of life's greatest gifts.

And she will name her Teruko, meaning "to shine."

With her whole heart and soul,

she will LOVE.

As the wind, sky, and waves meet,
Keiko shares her hopes for Teruko.

"And now, little one, I believe in you.

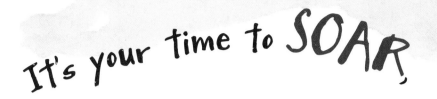

It's your time to SOAR, to SHINE and be FREE."

AUTHOR'S NOTE

Do you ever feel invisible or that your voice cannot be heard? Growing up as a young Asian American girl in a Los Angeles suburb, I often felt this way simply because I looked different than most of my neighbors. Now I'm a mother, and I want my daughters to have a better experience. As I searched for books for them, I was surprised by how few represented Asian Americans. All these reasons compelled me to write about a girl who shared some of my struggles but overcame them and learned how bright she could shine—one of my hopes for my daughters and for all little girls.

I am a sansei, or third-generation Japanese American. Although I grew up in America, my parents felt it was very important to expose us to Japanese culture too. On Sundays we went to a predominately Japanese church and signed up to play basketball for SEYO, a Japanese sports club. We often attended seasonal Japanese festivals such as Obon, which is about honoring one's ancestors, and the cherry blossom festivals in LA's Little Tokyo neighborhood. These were pockets in time where I felt I truly fit in as I'd be with other young girls who looked like me and understood what I did.

Working hard and not complaining or expressing opinions that draw attention to ourselves is deeply rooted in Asian culture. My dear Bachan (another way to say "*obaachan*" or "grandmother") used to say "*gaman.*" It means to be patient, persevere, or be tolerant. Because of this, writing a story that reflected aspects of my life was difficult; I'm not used to being so open about my own story.

If you are a minority or someone who feels different, role models are important. I wanted to show Keiko as president so kids could see a strong minority woman in this important role. The phrases at the end of each scene, such as "She is kind," are part of Keiko's journey, but they also embody a person striving to do their best. I included them because using courage, kindness, perseverance, inspiration, hope, and love reflects something positive we can all aspire to.

My Watari family crest appears throughout the book as do origami pieces, which represent different parts of Keiko's life. Teruko, Keiko's daughter, is named

after me. Teruko, which is my middle name, means "to illuminate or shine" in Japanese. Since understanding that you can shine is central to the story, it seemed the perfect fit.

Thank you for coming along on Keiko's journey. My hope is that young girls such as my daughters might see themselves in Keiko and be inspired to become whatever they dream. To them I say: Find your own voice and share it. And remember that no matter what someone might tell you or think, you will always shine brightly.

—Korey Watari

I WANTED TO SHARE MORE ABOUT A FEW ASPECTS OF JAPANESE LIFE REFLECTED IN THE BOOK.

Origami—This is the Japanese art of paper folding that has been around since the sixth century. Origami paper is often bright and features beautiful designs on the front and back. As a child, I made origami with my sisters, and now as a mother I fold it with my daughters, one way I'm passing along my Japanese heritage.

The crane—The crane is a bird, called *tsuru* in Japanese, that's a symbol of success and good fortune in Japanese culture. When a crane is folded into origami, it is believed that one's heart's desire will come true. My sisters, cousins, uncle, and I actually folded one thousand cranes for my parents' twenty-fifth wedding anniversary to wish them eternal happiness and love. Cranes are shown throughout this book because they represent Keiko's hope that she'll fulfill her dreams.

Kamon—A family crest, also called *mon*. This is a Japanese symbol of each family's origins or lineage. My family's crest, pictured here, is featured in a few places in the book. Can you find it?

Kimono—This is a traditional Japanese garment or robe with wide sleeves, wrapped in the front and fastened with a wide sash called an *obi*. Keiko wears one when dancing at the Obon festival with her newly discovered ballet friends. When I was young, I used to play and have adventures in an old vintage kimono my mother gave me. That's me in the photo on the facing page.

Bento box—A home-packed meal of Japanese origin. Keiko has one in the lunchroom scene. My mom used to make a bento of chicken teriyaki and Furikake onigiris, or rice balls with seasoning. We still enjoy them!